FUNKY CLUB PRESENTS...

Disco DONKEY

BOOK NOW!

This igloo book belongs to...

....

BUMP, HUSTLE AND
groove
WITH THE
HOTTEST STAR
IN TOWN!

igloobooks

Published in 2022
First published in the UK by Igloo Books Ltd
An imprint of Igloo Books Ltd
Cottage Farm, NN6 0BJ, UK
Owned by Bonnier Books
Sveavägen 56, Stockholm, Sweden
www.igloobooks.com

1122 004
4 6 8 10 9 7 5
ISBN 978-1-80022-677-7

Written by Everley Hart
Illustrated by Mike Byrne

Designed by Justine Ablett
Edited by Stephanie Moss

Printed and manufactured in China

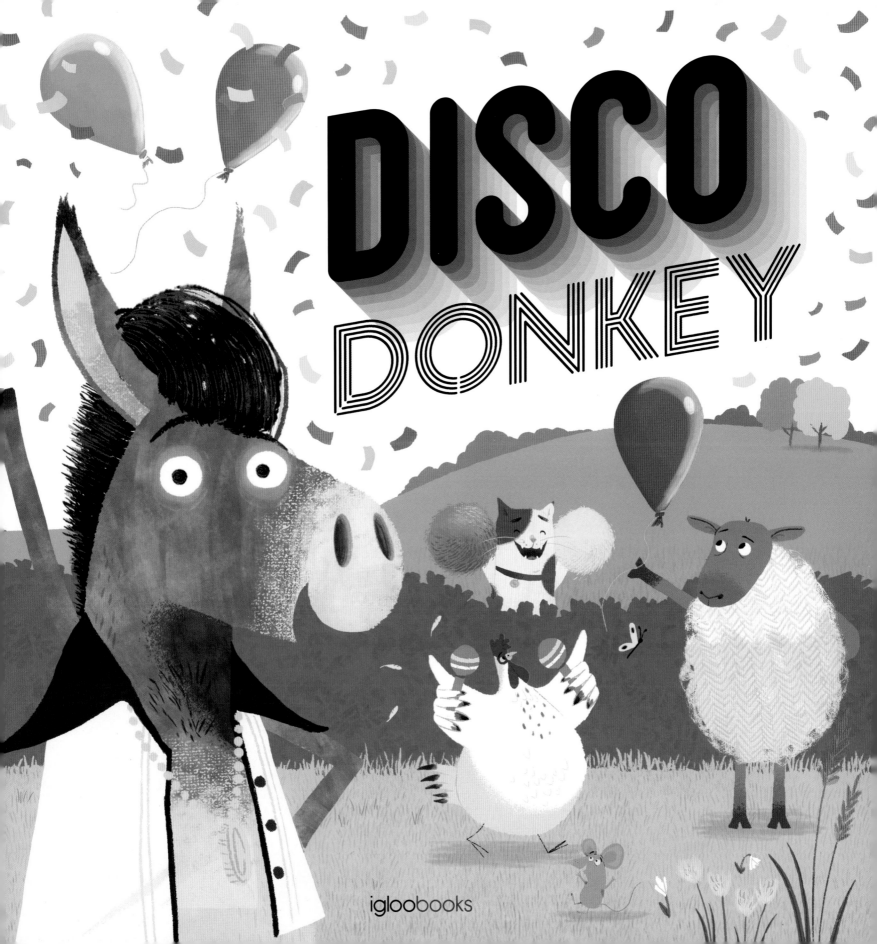

DISCO
DONKEY

igloobooks

Tell me, have you seen before,
upon a light-up disco floor,
a donkey funky dancing
as he's singing out...

HEE HAW!

The animals all frown
while yawning,

Donkey, turn it down!
Your parties are so loud they
wake up everyone in town.

They're up all night, awake,
so sleepy that they make mistakes.

Donkey, stop the discos,

they plead.

His friends sleep in till three, then look around and shout, **YIPPEE!**

No more midnight music,

they say.

Finally, we're free!

Of course, it isn't long before they miss his disco songs.

They wake up every night and wish their donkey wasn't gone.

Meanwhile, to his surprise,
Donkey's fame is on the rise!

He has so many fans, he needs
to dress up in disguise.

How they all delight as
Donkey dances every night.
He bumps and grooves...

... and hustles
under flashing
DISCO
lights.

The crowd is always near as they YELL and WHOOP and cheer.

They follow him all day until he wants to disappear.

He sniffs, "It's really tough to cope with all this stardom stuff.
I wish I could go home, but all my friends have had enough."

So, Donkey makes a plan to help escape his screaming fans.

I'll stop my disco moves and look as foolish as I can!

His arms **flap** in the air,

his **KNEES-A-KNOCKING** everywhere.

He **SWIVELS** in a circle,
while the crowd begins to stare.

They'll leave now, Donkey's sure.
But all his fans scream out...

He knows what he must do when they all flap and **WIGGLE** too.

The crowd goes
wild and shouts,

We want to
DISCO
just like you!

And so, he sneaks away to find another place to stay.

Donkey moves in shadows, till he hears somebody say...

It's Donkey!

Then he groans as they snap selfies on their phones.

Then, suddenly a crowd chases him all the way back...

They turn around and leave at last,
and Donkey feels proud.

We want to make amends,

say all his sorry farmyard friends.

Does our star forgive them?
Well, let's see how this one ends!

The piglets pirouette,
the tango turkeys start to sweat.

The hip-hop horses break dance
at their best dance party yet!